Dear God,
Mrs. Green needs your help. Could you help get Patches out of the tree?
Love,
Tyler

...nd Patches
...as purring real loud.
Love,
Tyler

...you for
...the great day! I won
the game!
Love,
Tyler

Dear God,
I went fishing with Grandpa and caught a big fish!
Love,
Tyler

Dear God,
I need your help to find my Special,
...ove
...yler

Dear God,
...o you think you
...uld help me clean
...room? My Mom
...it's a real mess!
...ove
...Tyler

Dear God,
I think Sam and Mrs. Green are going to write you letters too!
Love,
Tyler

Dear God,
Sam said her Dad could use help to find his!
Love,
...yler

Dear God,
I looked in the sky and saw another rainbow today!
Love,
Tyler

...God,
...e you could
...my brother
...stop being a pest.
Love,
Tyler

Dear God,
Could you please he...
get...

Dear God,
Thank you for my family and friends!
Love,
Tyler
P.S. Even my little brother.

To the Almighty Father, without Him I am nothing. For Tyler, the reason I have God in my life. For Savanah and Brendan's unconditional love, mom and dad for standing by me, and my Patrick for allowing me to be part of Tyler's life and continuing the journey.
—H.D.

For Tyler, without him there would be no story. For Heather, Brendan, and Savanah's patience.
For my parents, brothers, and family—and for the glory of God and His Kingdom.
—P.D.

For Lee, thank you for understanding the late nights, long weekends, and popcorn dinners.
—T.L.

ZONDERKIDZ

Letters to God
Copyright © 2010 by Patrick and Heather Doughtie
Illustrations © 2010 by Tammie Lyon

Requests for information should be addressed to:
Zonderkidz, *Grand Rapids, Michigan 49530*

ISBN: 978-0310-72013-3

Editor: Barbara Herndon
Art direction and design: Mary pat Pino
Cover design: Extra Credit Projects

Printed in China

10 11 12 13 14 15 / LPC / 6 5 4 3 2 1

letters to God

Written by Patrick and Heather Doughtie

Illustrated by Tammie Lyon

ZONDERVAN.com/
AUTHORTRACKER
follow your favorite authors

This morning I woke up excited. My fishing trip with Grandpa was only two days away!

I had to find my special compass that he gave me. It helps us find the hidden lake where we catch the big fish.

So I looked...

and looked...

but I couldn't find it.

"You need to clean your room or no trip this weekend," Mom said. But I had to find my compass!

Dad always says that if I have a problem, I should talk to God about it.

"HEY, GOD. CAN YOU PLEASE HELP ME FIND MY COMPASS?"

I waited. Then I looked some more. I still couldn't find it.

I thought maybe God didn't hear me,
so I decided to write him a letter.
Everyone likes to get mail!

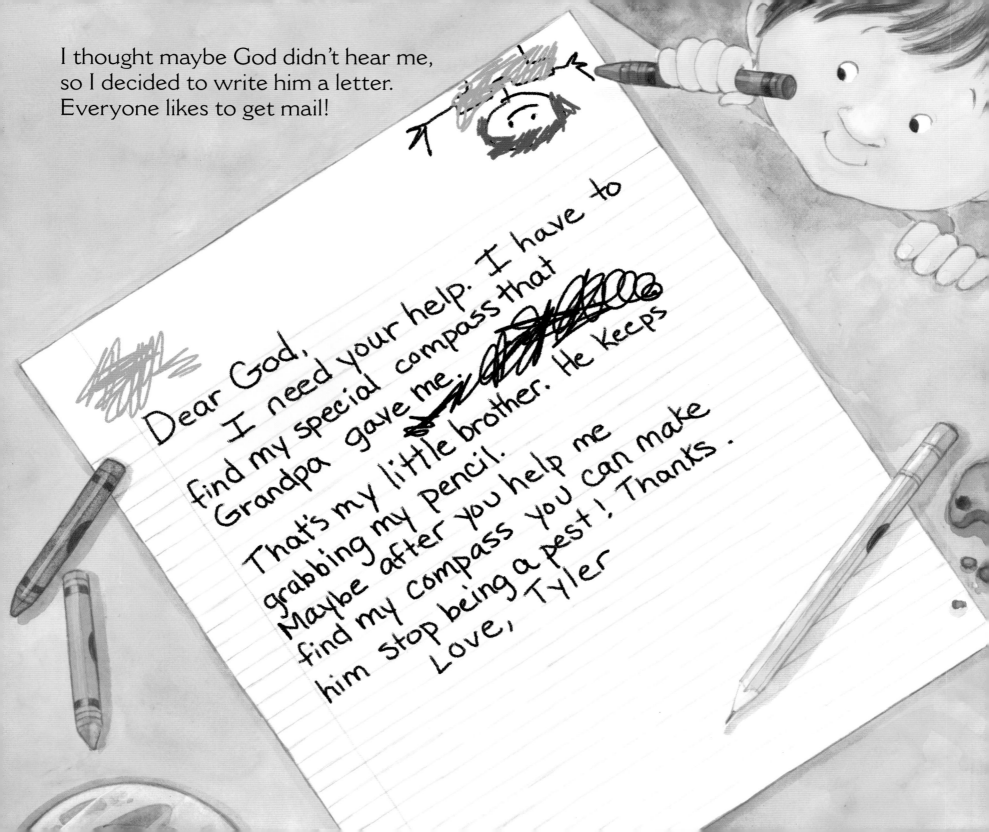

Dear God,
I need your help. I have to find my special compass that Grandpa gave me. ~~...~~ That's my little brother. He keeps grabbing my pencil. Maybe after you help me find my compass you can make him stop being a pest! Thanks.
Love, Tyler

I put the letter in an envelope. I didn't have God's address, but I figured the mailman would know it.

On my way to the mailbox, I saw Mrs. Green looking up in her tree. Patches was stuck and wouldn't come down.

I told her she should write a letter to God and ask for help. "That's a very good idea," she said.

find my spe... Grandpa gave...

Thats my little bro... grabbing my pencil. Maybe after you help me find my compass you can make him stop being a pest! Thanks. Love, Tyler

P. S. One more thing, God. Please help Patches get down from the tree. He looks really scared.

I had another idea. I opened my envelope and asked God to help Patches *for* Mrs. Green.

Down the street I saw my best friend, Sam. She seemed sad.
"My dad lost his job," she said. "We might have to move!" I told her
maybe God could help and that she should write him a letter.

Since I was on my way to drop off *my* letter, I opened it again and added a note for Sam.

I finally made it to the mailbox. Just before I put the letter inside, I saw a big rainbow across the sky. I think God put that there just for me.

On my way home, I saw Sam kicking a soccer ball with her dad. They were laughing and having fun.

And Mrs. Green was hugging Patches.

When I got home I still had to clean my room. So I cleaned...

and cleaned...

and guess what I found?

My compass!
I was so happy I decided to
write God another letter.

Dear God, if I had listened to I guess if I had listened to my mom and cleaned my room, I would have found my compass earlier. But, then I wouldn't have been able to write you about Mrs. Green and Sam.

Thank you for letting me find my compass, and for Sam getting to spend time with her dad, and for helping Patches out of the tree.

And about my little brother... I guess some things take more time.

Love, Tyler

P.S. I think I'll write again tomorrow.

Use the stationery in the back of this book to write your own letter to God.

Tyler Doughtie was born in Nashville, Tennessee, September 23, 1995. He was a loving and much-loved son, brother, and friend with a huge heart for God. He excelled at soccer but enjoyed all sports, outdoor activities, and games. Tyler prided himself in academics and was involved in Cub Scouts and AWANA. He wanted to be a carpenter like his father when he grew up, until he saw professional soccer player, Landon Donovan, on the cover of a sports magazine and learned that he could get paid to play soccer, his true love.

In January 2003, Tyler was diagnosed with Medulloblastoma, a rare childhood brain tumor. He bravely underwent treatment and surgery to remove the tumor but, after a short remission, passed away on March 7, 2005. While boxing things up from his room more than two years after Tyler's death, his dad Patrick found letters that his son had written to God while he was ill. Tyler's story and these very special letters became the inspiration for the film *Letters to God*.

Tyler is greatly missed, but his legacy lives on through this story about child-like faith and trust in God.

Dear God,
Mrs. Green needs your help. Could you help get Patches out of the tree?
Love
Tyler

...was purring real loud.
Love,
Tyler

...and Patches

...hank you for the great day! I won the game!
Love,
Tyler

...ear God,

Dear God,
I went fishing with Grandpa and caught a big fish!
Love,
Tyler

Dear God,
I need your help to find my special.
Love
Tyler

Dear God,
Do you think you could help me clean my room? My Mom said it's a real mess!
Love
Tyler

Dear God,
I think Sam and Mrs. Green are going to write you letters too!
Love,
Tyler

Dear God,
Sam said her Dad could use help to find his...
Love,
Tyler

Dear God,
I looked in the sky and saw another rainbow today!
Love,
Tyler

Dear God,
Maybe you could help my brother stop being a pest.
Love,
Tyler

Dear God,
Thank you for my family and friends.
Love,
Tyler
P.S. Even my little brother.

Dear God,
Could you please he...